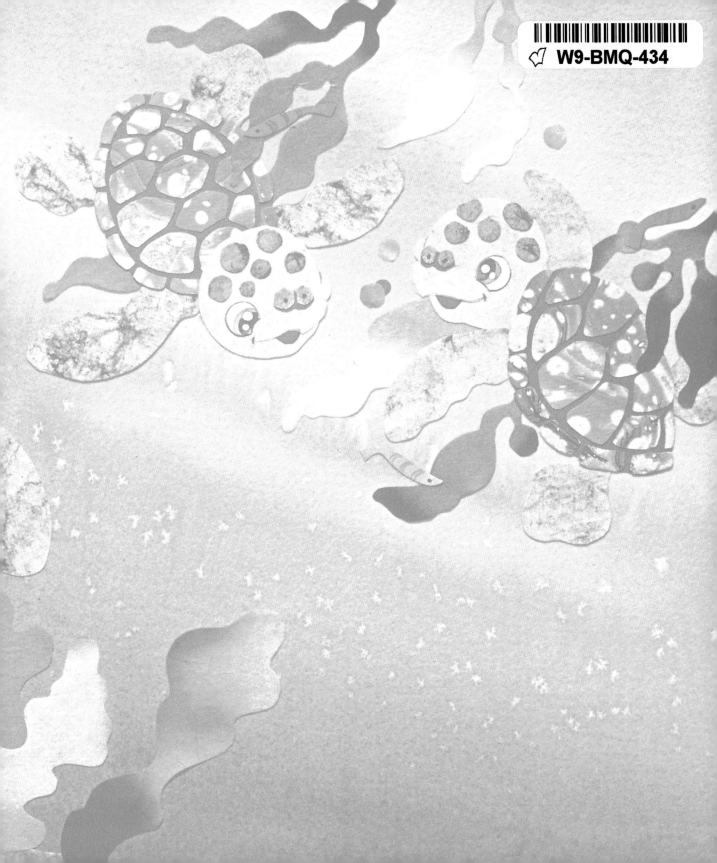

Over on the Island

written by Yuko Green and Sarah Tupou

illustrated by Yuko Green

ISLAND HERITAGE™
PUBLISHING

Published by

ISLAND HERITAGE™
P U B L I S H I N G
A DIVISION OF THE MADDEN CORPORATION
94-411 KŌʻAKI STREET, WAIPAHU, HAWAIʻI 96797-2806
PHONE: (800) 468-2800 • FAX (808) 564-8877
islandheritage.com

ISBN# 1-59700-280-1

First Edition, First Printing - 2007

For my girls, Kaiona, Malie & Kianapauka–
Keep discovering, exploring, learning . . . Read!
Love, S.T.

For Eve and Daisy with aloha–
Your home is always here
over on the island.
- Y.G.

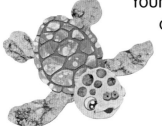

4

Over on the island,
in the soft morning sun,
lived a proud mother whale
and her little whale one.
"Splash!" said the mother.
"I splash," said the one.
So he splashed with his tail
in the soft morning sun.

5

Over on the island,
in the ocean clear and blue,
lived a wise mother turtle
and her little turtles two.
"Paddle!" said the mother.
"We paddle," said the two.
So they paddled and they floated
in the ocean clear and blue.

8

Over on the island,
by a coconut tree,
lived a noisy mother myna
and her little myna three.
"Squawk!" said the mother.
"We squawk," said the three.
So they squawked and were happy
by the coconut tree.

Over on the island,
on a white sandy shore,
lived a mother ghost crab
and her little crabbies four.
"Dig!" said the mother.
"We dig," said the four.
So they dug and they scurried
on the white sandy shore.

Over on the island,
where the swimmers jump and dive,
lived a nervous mother fish
and her little fishies five.
"Dart!" said the mother.
"We dart," said the five.
So they darted and they swam
where the swimmers jump and dive.

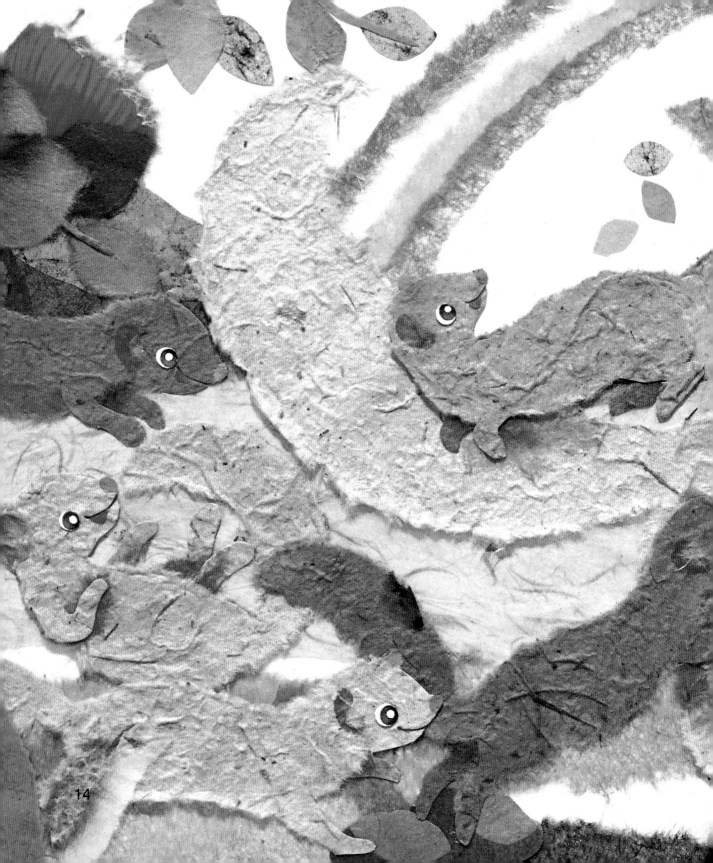

Over on the island,
in the reeds and the sticks,
lived a mother mongoose
and her little mongoose six.
"Scamper!" said the mother.
"We scamper," said the six.
So they scampered and they ran
in the reeds and the sticks.

15

Over on the island,
in a bright coral heaven,
lived a mother jellyfish
and her little jellies seven.
"Bloop!" said the mother.
"We bloop," said the seven.
So they blooped all around
in the bright coral heaven.

Over on the island,
as the day turned late,
lived a blue mother dolphin
and her little dolphins eight.
"Leap!" said the mother.
"We leap," said the eight.
So they leapt and they twirled
as the day turned late.

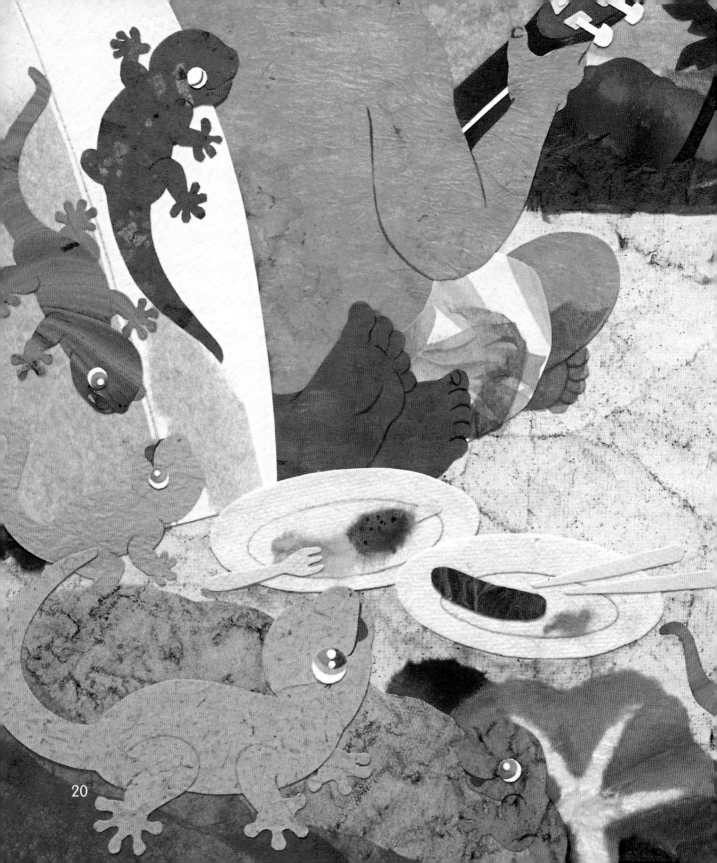

Over on the island,
where the surfers sit to dine,
lived a feisty mother gecko
and her little geckos nine.
"Sing!" said the mother.
"We sing," said the nine.
So they sang and they danced
where the surfers sit to dine.

Over on the island,
in a cozy coral den,
lived a mother starfish
and her little starfish ten.
"Stretch!" said the mother.
"We stretch," said the ten.
So they stretched and they yawned
in their cozy coral den.

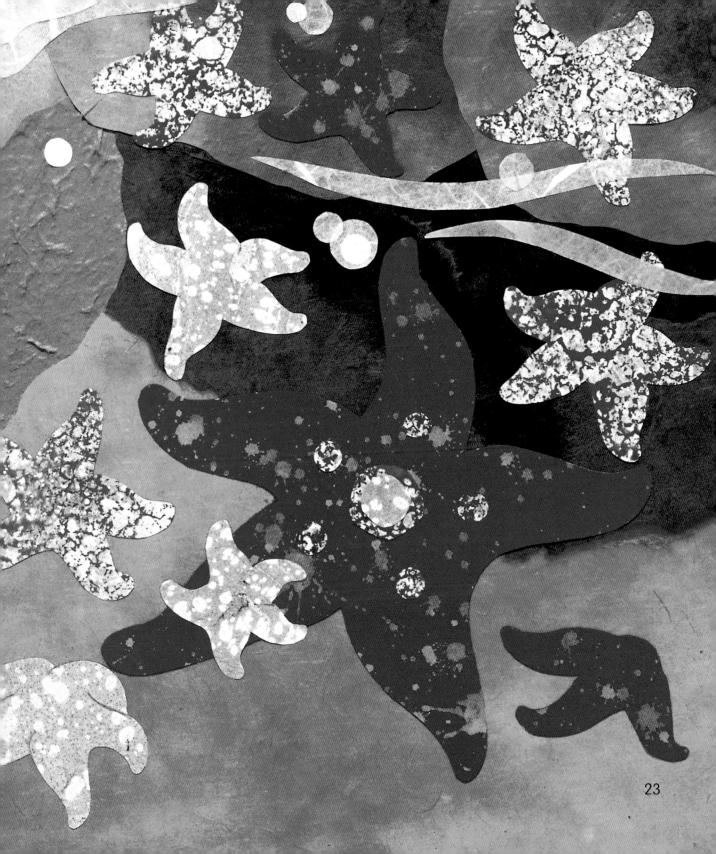

THE END

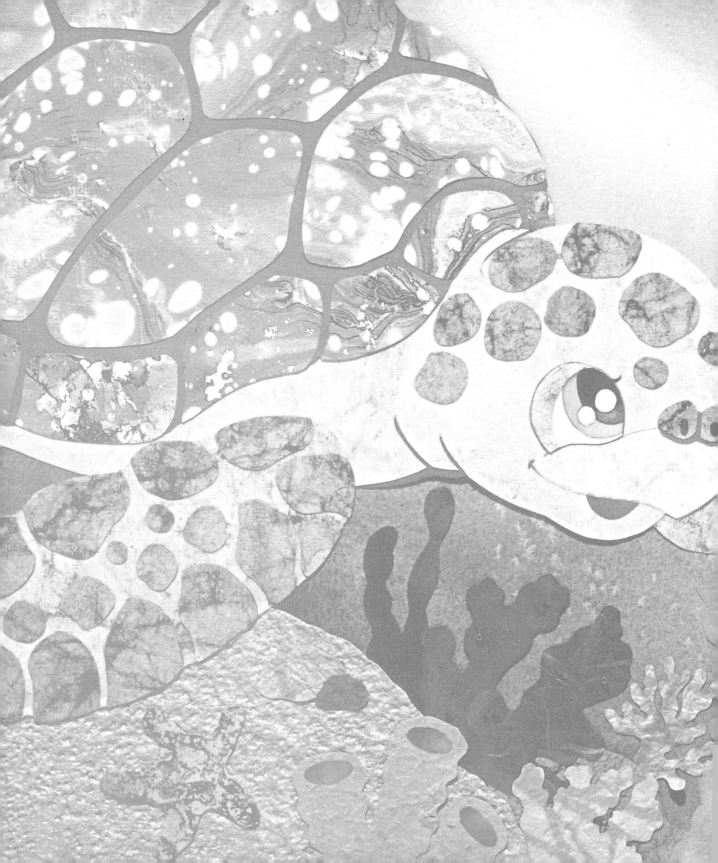